FLIGHT

⊚ OF THE ⊚

DODO

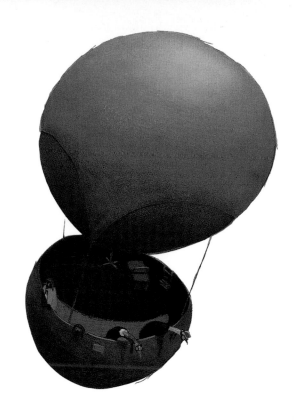

PETER BROWN

LITTLE, BROWN AND COMPANY

New York ⇝ Boston

For Alvina and Tracy.
Two of my favorite birds.

Little, Brown and Company

Time Warner Book Group
1271 Avenue of the Americas, New York, NY 10020
Visit our Web site at www.lb-kids.com

First Edition: October 2005

Library of Congress Cataloging-in-Publication Data

Brown, Peter.
 Flight of the Dodo / Peter Brown.— 1st ed.
  p. cm.
 Summary: Penguin and his other flightless bird friends invent a flying machine,
but they fly right into a thunderstorm.
 ISBN 0-316-11038-8
 〚1. Flightless birds—Fiction. 2. Flight—Fiction. 3. Thunderstorms—Fiction.〛
I. Title.
PZ7.B81668Fl 2005
〚E〛—dc22

2004004711

10 9 8 7 6 5 4 3 2 1

SC

Book design by Tracy Shaw

Manufactured in China

The illustrations for this book were done in acrylic and pencil on board.
The text was set in Kennerly, and the display type is Klepto.

NO PENGUINS WERE POOPED ON IN THE MAKING OF THIS BOOK.

It was a beautiful morning, and Penguin was feeling good.

But just when he waddled outside . . .

SPLAT!!!

A goose pooped on Penguin.

"For crying out loud!" he screeched as the goose flapped away.
"If I could fly I'd at least watch where I pooped!"

But Penguin couldn't fly. He was just a flightless bird.

He was a Waddler.

Penguin had always dreamed of flying, and it didn't
seem fair to him that the Flappers got to have all the fun.
So he rounded up his friends to discuss the future of
the Waddlers.

"Ostrich, Kiwi, Cassowary: We are all birds, but have any of us ever had a bird's-eye view of anything?"

"Don't be silly!" Ostrich laughed. "Waddlers can't fly. Only a Flapper can have a bird's-eye view."

"That's been true for the last fifty gazillion years," said Penguin, "but this stain on my jacket says it's time for change!"

The more Penguin squawked about flying and seeing the world, the more sense he made to his friends. And before long they came to an agreement. The Waddlers were going to fly. They just had to figure out how.

Inventing a flying machine wasn't easy,
and the Waddlers tried one lousy idea . . .

after another.

But after months of slaving away, they finally came up with something they thought just might work. They called it the *Dodo*. The Waddlers said good-bye to the ground for the first time in their lives, and climbed in.

Three . . . two . . . one . . . LIFTOFF!

Up they went above the trees, over the hilltops, and through the clouds, until the *waddling* birds were flying higher than the *flapping* birds!

"I've never seen so much stuff before!" Cassowary squawked.

"We didn't even flap our wings once," said Penguin. "Those Flappers are doing it all wrong!"

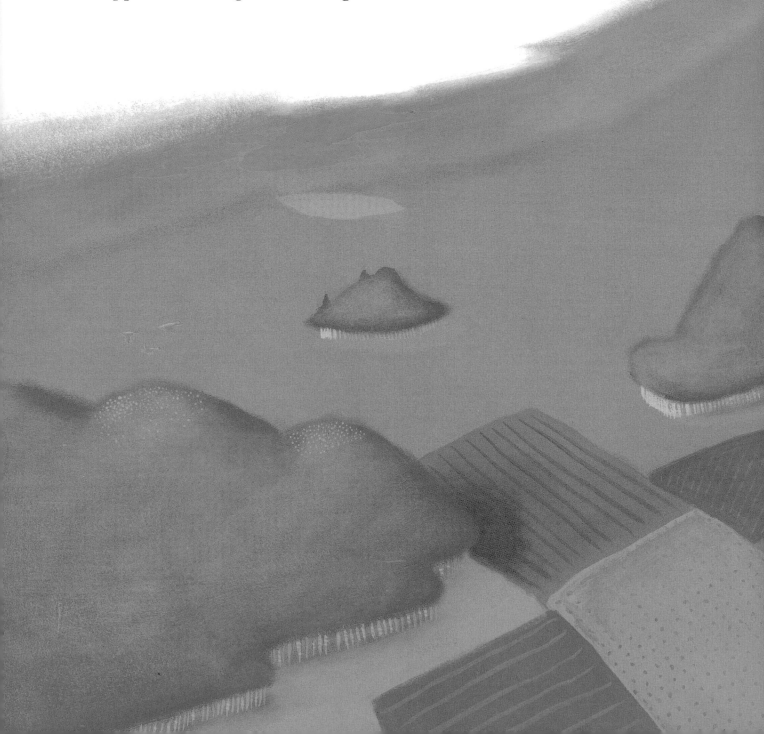

The Waddlers had waited their whole lives to get off the ground.
And now that they'd actually done it, there were a few things they
wanted to try.

At last Kiwi could do the ultimate cannonball.

Cassowary wondered what fluffy white clouds tasted like.

Ostrich had heard that fly-fishing was fun,
but had no idea how to do it.

When the *Dodo* drifted over a lonely old rock, Penguin finally felt the thrill of target pooping.

One thing *all* the Waddlers wanted to do was show the world that they were now officially airborne. And when they heard the flock of geese honking proudly in the distance, the Waddlers knew it was time to make their grand appearance.

Penguin flew the Dodo below the geese and above the geese,

and tried every ballooning stunt his bird brain could think up!

After each trick his co-pilots turned a more disgusting shade of green.

"I don't think this is such a good idea," whined Ostrich as his stomach groaned.

But that didn't stop Penguin. He raced past the geese, laughing.

"Last ones to that cloud are a flock of geese!"

The geese didn't even try to keep up. Instead they sank below the *Dodo* and disappeared.

Penguin was feeling quite pleased with himself when suddenly he heard a loud rumbling sound. He looked ahead of the *Dodo* and realized that they were racing straight toward a thunderstorm! He turned the *Dodo* around, but within seconds dark clouds surrounded them and rain began pouring down.

They pulled levers and tightened ropes, but the storm was too strong. The Waddlers had no control of the *Dodo*.

"We don't belong in the sky!" cried Cassowary.

"What were we thinking?"

Just as the other Waddlers were about to really lose it, Penguin saw something. Below the clouds and through the rain Penguin was barely able to spot the flock of geese sitting safely on the ground. He needed their help. But the geese were too far below to hear the squawking Waddlers. There was only one way to get their attention.

After factoring in the rain and wind and position of the *Dodo*, Penguin let loose the most precisely aimed poop ever to fall from the sky.

The geese took flight to investigate the source of the poop and were soon flapping alongside the *Dodo*.

"We just want to go home," squawked Penguin. "Please help us!"

One look at the frazzled Waddlers and the kindhearted geese knew just what to do.

The *Dodo* was big and heavy, and the storm was strong,
but those geese flapped like they'd never flapped before.
Very slowly they came out from the storm, and very slowly
the Waddlers began to feel safe again.

With a **THUD** the *Dodo* finally landed,
and the Waddlers' first flight was over.

It was clear that the Waddlers had a lot to learn about flying. And it was clear to Penguin that the geese had a few things to learn as well. After teaching each other some very important lessons, the Waddlers and geese became good friends.

With heads full of flying facts, and all bottoms aiming accurately, the Waddlers cruised through the sky on the next flight of the *Dodo*.